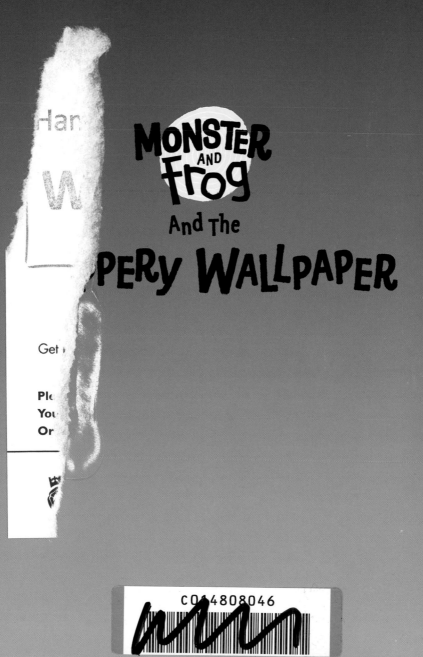

MONSTER AND Frog

And The

...PERY WALLPAPER

For George

R.I.

For Loveday

R.A.

Consultant: Prue Goodwin,
Lecturer in literacy and children's books,
University of Reading

ORCHARD BOOKS
338 Euston Road, London NW1 3BH
Orchard Books Australia
Hachette Children's Books
Level 17/207 Kent Street, Sydney NSW 2000

First published in Great Britain in 2006
First paperback publication 2007

Text © Rose Impey 2006
Illustrations © Russell Ayto 2006

The rights of Rose Impey to be identified as the author and
Russell Ayto to be identified as the illustrator of this Work
have been asserted by them in accordance with the
Copyright, Designs and Patents Act, 1988.

A CIP catalogue record for this book is available from the British Library

ISBN 1 84121 540 6 (hardback)
ISBN 1 84362 230 0 (paperback)

3 5 7 9 10 8 6 4 2

Printed in China

MONSTER AND Frog

And The

SLIPPERY WALLPAPER

ROSE IMPEY ☙ RUSSELL AYTO

ORCHARD BOOKS

It is time for Monster to
spring-clean his house.

"This house needs more than
a spring-clean," says Frog.

"This house needs painting
and decorating."

Monster has never done any
decorating before.

Luckily Frog knows all about decorating.

"First you need to move the
furniture," says Frog.
"I will help."

Frog tells Monster where to move
the table and chairs . . .

and the
TV . . .

and the sofa . . .

and the carpet and the rug. Phew!

Frog is very good at helping.

"Next," Frog says, "you must choose the paint and wallpaper. How about green?"
Monster does not really like green.

But green is Frog's favourite
colour.
"Trust me," says Frog. "I am
an expert on colours."

They start with the ceiling.

Frog tells Monster to hold
the ladder while he does
the painting.

Monster feels something dripping
on his head.
"Is it raining?" he asks Frog.

Frog leans over to wipe the paint
off Monster's head.
He leans too far.

Oops!

"Just look at my floor!"
groans Monster.

"Do not worry," says Frog.
"I have a great idea."

Now Monster has a green
floor too.
And he still does not like green.

It is time to hang the wallpaper.
Monster has never hung
wallpaper before.

"Leave it to me," says Frog.
"Wallpapering is what I do best."

Frog mixes the paste.

He spreads the paste on
the wallpaper.

Then he climbs
up the ladder.

But the wallpaper is so slippery it slides through Frog's fingers.

It lands on Monster's head.
He is covered in sticky paste.

"Just practising," says Frog.

This time Frog spreads the paste
on the wall.
He sticks the wallpaper to it.

"Easy-peasy," Frog tells Monster.
"I could do this with my
eyes shut."

Monster does not like the sound
of that.

When Frog has finished, it
looks as if he *has* done the whole
room with his eyes shut.

"I do not think that is right,"
says Monster.

"Hmmm," says Frog.
"Wallpapering is not as easy
as it looks."

He tells Monster to go and make a cup of tea while he puts things right.

But Monster cannot make a cup
of tea. He cannot even find
the kitchen.

Monster looks very sad.
He does not like this green house.
He wants his old house back.

He wants his door and his windows.
Frog says, "I will soon find them.
I am an expert at finding doors."

Frog peels off the paper until he finds the door and the windows. Then he scrubs the walls to get the sticky paste off.

Now the walls look
nice and blue again.
Monster is happy. It looks just
like his old house, but cleaner.

Monster's sister calls round.
"How nice your house looks,"
she tells Monster.
"All it needed was a good
spring-clean."

"That is just what I told Monster,"
says Frog. "It is lucky I was here.
Spring-cleaning is my speciality."

MONSTER AND Frog

ROSE IMPEY 🐸 RUSSELL AYTO

Enjoy all these adventures with Monster and Frog!

Monster and Frog and the Big Adventure
ISBN 1 84362 228 9
Monster and Frog Get Fit
ISBN 1 84362 231 9
Monster and Frog and the Slippery Wallpaper
ISBN 1 84362 230 0
Monster and Frog Mind the Baby
ISBN 1 84362 232 7
Monster and Frog and the Terrible Toothache
ISBN 1 84362 227 0
Monster and Frog and the All-in-Together Cake
ISBN 1 84362 233 5
Monster and Frog and the Haunted Tent
ISBN 1 84362 229 7
Monster and Frog and the Magic Show
ISBN 1 84362 234 3

All priced at £4.99

Orchard Colour Crunchies are available from all good bookshops, or can be ordered
direct from the publisher: Orchard Books, PO BOX 29, Douglas IM99 1BQ
Credit card orders please telephone 01624 836000
or fax 01624 837033 or visit our Internet site: www.wattspub.co.uk
or e-mail: bookshop@enterprise.net for details.

To order please quote title, author and ISBN
and your full name and address.
Cheques and postal orders should be made payable to 'Bookpost plc.'
Postage and packing is FREE within the UK
(overseas customers should add £1.00 per book).

Prices and availability are subject to change.